A Book of NURSERY RIDDLES

JANE JOHNSON

HOUGHTON MIFFLIN COMPANY   BOSTON   1985

In marble walls as white as milk,
Lined with a skin as soft as silk,
Within a fountain crystal-clear,
A golden apple doth appear.
No doors there are to this stronghold,
Yet thieves break in and steal the gold.

Riddle me, riddle me ree,
A little man in a tree;
A stick in his hand,
A stone in his throat,
If you read me this riddle
I'll give you a groat.

As black as ink and isn't ink,
As white as milk and isn't milk,
As soft as silk and isn't silk,
And hops about like a filly-foal.

Magpie

As I was going o'er London Bridge,
I heard something crack;
Not a man in all England
Can mend that.

Clothed in yellow, red and green,
I prate before the king and queen;
Of neither house nor land possessed,
By lords and knights I am caressed.

In spring I look gay,
Decked in comely array,
In summer more clothing I wear;
When colder it grows,
I fling off my clothes,
And in winter quite naked appear.

Two brothers are we,
Great burdens we bear,
On which we are bitterly pressed;
The truth is to say,
We are full all the day,
And empty when we go to rest.

Purple, yellow, red and green,
The king cannot reach it, nor yet the queen;
Nor can Old Noll, whose power's so great:
Tell me this riddle while I count to eight.

Rainbow

Four stiff-standers,
Four dilly-danders,
Two lookers,
Two crookers,
And a wig-wag.

I'm called by the name of a man,
Yet am as little as a mouse;
When winter comes I love to be
With my red target near the house.

Robin

Flour of England, fruit of Spain,
Met together in a shower of rain;
Put in a bag, tied round with a string;
If you tell me this riddle,
I'll give you a ring.

White bird featherless
Flew from Paradise,
Pitched on the castle wall;
Along came Lord Landless,
Took it up handless,
And rode away horseless
To the King's white wall.

I have a little sister, they call her
Peep-Peep,
She wades the waters deep, deep, deep;
She climbs the mountains high, high, high;
Poor little creature she has but one eye.

Little Nancy Etticoat,
With a white petticoat,
And a red nose;
She has no feet or hands,
The longer she stands
The shorter she grows.

Formed long ago, yet made today,
Employed when others sleep;
What few would like to give away,
Nor any wish to keep.